To:

_____

From:

_____

Date:

_____

© 2011 Summerside Press™
Minneapolis, MN 55438
www.summersidepress.com

God Loves You

A *Pocket Inspirations* Book

ISBN 978-1-60936-121-1

Scripture references are from the following sources: The Holy Bible,
King James Version (KJV). The Holy Bible, New International
Version®, NIV®. Copyright © 1973, 1978, 1984 by Biblica, Inc.™
Used by permission of Zondervan. All rights reserved worldwide.
The New King James Version (NKJV). Copyright © 1982 by Thomas
Nelson, Inc. Used by permission. The New American Standard
Bible® (NASB), Copyright © 1960, 1962, 1963, 1968, 1971, 1972,
1973, 1975, 1977, 1995 by The Lockman Foundation. Used by
permission. The Holy Bible, New Living Translation (NLT),
copyright © 1996, 2004. Used by permission of Tyndale House
Publishers, Inc., Wheaton, Illinois. *The Message* (MSG). Copyright
© 1993, 1994, 1995, 1996, 2000, 2001, 2002 by Eugene Peterson.
Used by permission of NavPress, Colorado Springs, CO.

Excluding Scripture verses and deity pronouns, in some quotations
references to men and masculine pronouns have been replaced
with gender-neutral or feminine references. Additionally, in some
quotations we have carefully updated verb forms and wording that
may distract modern readers.

Compiled by Marilyn Jansen
Designed by Jeff and Lisa Franke

*Summerside Press™ is an inspirational publisher offering fresh,
irresistible books to uplift the heart and engage the mind.*

Printed in the USA.

God Loves You

A *Pocket Inspirations* book

summerside
PRESS

Contents

For Himself

Although it is good to think upon
the kindness of God, and to love Him
and worship Him for it; yet it is far better
to gaze upon the pure essence of Him and
to love Him and worship Him for Himself.

We desire many things, and God offers
us only one thing. He can offer us only one
thing—Himself. He has nothing else to give.
There is nothing else to give.

Peter Kreeft

The LORD alone shall be exalted.

Isaiah 2:11 KJV

We are of such value to God that He came
to live among us...and to guide us home.
He will go to any length to seek us,
even to being lifted high upon the cross
to draw us back to Himself. We can only
respond by loving God for His love.

CATHERINE OF SIENA

✝ ✝ ✝

*In the deepest heart of everyone,
God planted a longing for Himself as He is:
a God of love.*

EUGENIA PRICE

The end of prayer is that
I come to know God Himself.

OSWALD CHAMBERS

Countless Beauties

May God give you eyes to see beauty
only the heart can understand.

✠ ✠ ✠

*All the world is an utterance
of the Almighty. Its countless beauties,
its exquisite adaptations,
all speak to you of Him.*

PHILLIPS BROOKS

One thing I ask of the LORD, this is what I seek:
that I may dwell in the house of the LORD all the
days of my life, to gaze upon the beauty of the
LORD and to seek him in his temple.

PSALM 27:4 NIV

Though I have seen the oceans and mountains, though I have read great books and seen great works of art, though I have heard symphonies and tasted the best wines and foods, there is nothing greater or more beautiful than those people I love.

CHRISTOPHER DE VINCK

Worship the LORD in the splendor of his holiness.

PSALM 96:9 NIV

Not every day of our lives is overflowing with joy and celebration. But there are moments when our hearts nearly burst within us for the sheer joy of being alive. The first sight of our newborn babies, the warmth of love in another's eyes, the fresh scent of rain on a hot summer's eve—moments like these renew in us a heartfelt appreciation for life.

GWEN ELLIS

The Grace of God

But God, being rich in mercy, because of His
great love with which He loved us, even when
we were dead in our transgressions, made us
alive together with Christ (by grace you have
been saved), and raised us up with Him, and
seated us with Him in the heavenly places in
Christ Jesus, so that in the ages to come He
might show the surpassing riches of His grace in
kindness toward us in Christ Jesus. For by grace
you have been saved through faith; and that not
of yourselves, it is the gift of God; not as a result
of works, so that no one may boast. For we are
His workmanship, created in Christ Jesus for
good works, which God prepared beforehand so
that we would walk in them.

Ephesians 2:4–10 nasb

God's forgiveness and love exist for you
as if you were the only person on earth.

Cecil Osborne

For the LORD God is a sun and shield; the LORD
gives grace and glory; no good thing does He
withhold from those who walk uprightly.

PSALM 84:11 NASB

Grace means that God already loves us as
much as an infinite God can possibly love.

PHILIP YANCEY

✠ ✠ ✠

*By the grace of God I am what I am,
and his grace to me was not without effect.
No, I worked harder than all of them—yet
not I, but the grace of God that was with me.*

1 CORINTHIANS 15:10 NIV

Promise of Love

A rainbow stretches from one end of the sky to
the other. Each shade of color, each facet of light
displays the radiant spectrum of God's love:
a promise that He will always love each one
of us at our worst and at our best.

Faithful, O Lord, Thy mercies are,
A rock that cannot move!
A thousand promises declare
Thy constancy of love.

CHARLES WESLEY

May your unfailing love come to me, O LORD,
your salvation according to your promise.

PSALM 119:41 NIV

God's love never ceases. Never....
God doesn't love us less if we fail or more
if we succeed. God's love never ceases.

MAX LUCADO

✝ ✝ ✝

*God promises to love me all day,
sing songs all through the night!
My life is God's prayer.*

PSALM 42:8 MSG

God has not promised sun without rain,
joy without sorrow, peace without pain.
But God has promised strength for the day,
rest for the labor, light for the way,
grace for the trials, help from above,
unfailing sympathy, undying love.

ANNIE JOHNSON FLINT

God makes a promise—faith believes it, hope
anticipates it, patience quietly awaits it.

Tender Love

Love is the sweet, tender, melting nature of God
flowing into the creature, making the creature
most like unto Himself.

ISAAC PENINGTON

For the word of the LORD is right and true;
he is faithful in all he does.
The LORD loves righteousness and justice;
the earth is full of his unfailing love.

PSALM 33:4–5 NIV

One way to get comfort is to plead the promise
of God in prayer, show Him His handwriting;
God is tender of His Word.

THOMAS MANTON

For, lo, the winter is past, the rain is over
and gone; the flowers appear on the earth;
the time of the singing of birds is come….
Arise, my love, my fair one, and come away.

SONG OF SOLOMON 2:11–13 KJV

✦ ✦ ✦

LORD, don't hold back your tender mercies
from me.
Let your unfailing love and faithfulness
always protect me.

PSALM 40:11 NLT

He is everything that is good and comfortable
for us. He is our clothing that for love wraps us,
clasps us, and all surrounds us for tender love.

JULIAN OF NORWICH

May the Lord direct your hearts
into the love of God.

2 THESSALONIANS 3:5 NASB

The Goodness of God

The goodness of God is infinitely
more wonderful than we will
ever be able to comprehend.

A. W. Tozer

All that is good, all that is true,
all that is beautiful, all that is beneficent,
be it great or small, be it perfect
or fragmentary, natural as well as supernatural,
moral as well as material, comes from God.

John Henry Newman

We walk without fear, full of hope and courage
and strength to do His will, waiting for the
endless good which He is always giving as fast as
He can get us able to take it in.

George MacDonald

✢ ✢ ✢

*Open your mouth and taste,
open your eyes and see—how good GOD is.
Blessed are you who run to him.
Worship GOD if you want the best;
worship opens doors to all his goodness.*

PSALM 34:8–9 MSG

Our greatness rests solely on the fact that God in His incomprehensible goodness has bestowed His love upon us. God does not love us because we are so valuable; we are valuable because God loves us.

HELMUT THIELICKE

Savor little glimpses of God's goodness and His majesty, thankful for the gift of them: winding pathways through the woods, a bright green canopy overhead, and dappled sunshine falling all around, warm upon our faces.

The Majesty of God

O LORD, our Lord, how majestic is your name
in all the earth! You have set your glory above
the heavens.... When I consider your heavens,
the work of your fingers, the moon and the
stars, which you have set in place, what is man
that you are mindful of him, the son of man
that you care for him? You made him a little
lower than the heavenly beings and crowned
him with glory and honor.... O LORD, our Lord,
how majestic is your name in all the earth!

PSALM 8:1, 3–5, 9 NIV

✝ ✝ ✝

*For God is, indeed, a wonderful Father
who longs to pour out His mercy upon us,
and whose majesty is so great that He can
transform us from deep within.*

TERESA OF AVILA

Yours, O Lord, is the greatness and the
power and the glory and the majesty
and the splendor, for everything in heaven
and earth is yours. Yours, O Lord, is the kingdom;
you are exalted as head over all.

1 CHRONICLES 29:11 NIV

Let every kindred, every tribe,
On this terrestial ball,
To Him all majesty ascribe,
And crown Him Lord of all.

EDWARD PERRONET

Search high and low, scan skies and land,
you'll find nothing and no one quite like GOD.
The holy angels are in awe before him; he looms
immense and august over everyone around him.
GOD-of-the-Angel-Armies, who is like you,
powerful and faithful from every angle?

PSALM 89:6–8 MSG

Morning and Evening

We are silent at the beginning of the day
because God should have the first word,
and we are silent before going to sleep because
the last word also belongs to God.... O Lord
my God, thank You for bringing this day
to a close; thank You for giving me rest
in body and soul. Your hand has been over me
and has guarded and preserved me.

DIETRICH BONHOEFFER

✛ ✛ ✛

*God loves you in the morning sun and
the evening rain, without caution or regret.*

BRENNAN MANNING

May none of God's wonderful works keep silent,
night or morning. Bright stars, high mountains,
the depths of the seas, sources of rushing rivers:
May all of these break into song to God, the
only Lord of love. And all the angels in the
heavens reply: May power, praise, honor, and
eternal glory be to God, the only Giver of grace.

Where morning dawns and evening
fades you call forth songs of joy.

PSALM 65:8 NIV

All the absurd little meetings, decisions,
and skirmishes that go to make up our days.
It all adds up to very little, and yet it all adds
up to very much. Our days are full
of nonsense, and yet not, because it is precisely
into the nonsense of our days that God speaks
to us words of great significance.

FREDERICK BUECHNER

In the morning let our hearts gaze upon
God's love...and in the beauty of that vision,
let us go forth to meet the day.

ROY LESSIN

It is good to give thanks to the LORD and to sing
praises to Your name, O Most High;
to declare Your lovingkindness in the morning and
Your faithfulness by night.

PSALM 92:1–2 NASB

The Faithfulness of God

You, O God, are both tender and kind,
not easily angered, immense in love,
and you never, never quit.

PSALM 86:15 MSG

God takes care of His own.... At just the
right moment He steps in and proves
Himself as our faithful heavenly Father.

CHARLES R. SWINDOLL

✝ ✝ ✝

*For your unfailing love is as high
as the heavens. Your faithfulness reaches
to the clouds. Be exalted, O God,
above the highest heavens. May your
glory shine over all the earth.*

PSALM 57:10–11 NLT

Be assured, if you walk with Him and look to Him
and expect help from Him, He will never fail you.

GEORGE MÜLLER

Let the morning bring me word of your
unfailing love, for I have put my trust in you.

PSALM 143:8 NIV

Regardless of whether we feel strong or weak in
our faith, we remember that our assurance
is not based upon our ability to conjure up
some special feeling. Rather, it is built upon
a confident assurance in the faithfulness of God.
We focus on His trustworthiness
and especially on His steadfast love.

RICHARD J. FOSTER

The LORD is righteous...He will do
no injustice. Every morning He brings
His justice to light; He does not fail.

ZEPHANIAH 3:5 NASB

Made for Joy

Our hearts were made for joy. Our hearts
were made to enjoy the One who created them.
Too deeply planted to be much affected by
the ups and downs of life, this joy is a knowing
and a being known by our Creator.
He sets our hearts alight with radiant joy.

If one is joyful, it means that one
is faithfully living for God, and that
nothing else counts; and if one gives joy
to others one is doing God's work.
With joy without and joy within, all is well.

JANET ERSKINE STUART

✤ ✤ ✤

The joy of the LORD is your strength.

NEHEMIAH 8:10 KJV

Live for today but hold your hands open to tomorrow. Anticipate the future and its changes with joy. There is a seed of God's love in every event, every circumstance, every unpleasant situation in which you may find yourself.

BARBARA JOHNSON

Always be full of joy in the Lord.
I say it again—rejoice!

PHILIPPIANS 4:4 NLT

I have known the other joys of life, I suppose, as much as most men; I have known art and beauty, music and gladness; I have known friendship and love and family ties; but it is certain that till we see GOD in the world—GOD in the bright and boundless universe—we never know the highest joy.

ORVILLE DEWEY

Fruit in Season

What happens when we live God's way?
He brings gifts into our lives, much
the same way that fruit appears in an
orchard—things like affection for others,
exuberance about life, serenity. We develop
a willingness to stick with things, a sense of
compassion in the heart, and a conviction that
a basic holiness permeates things and people.

GALATIANS 5:22–23 MSG

Sometimes our fate resembles a fruit
tree in winter. Who would think that
those branches would turn green again
and blossom, but we hope it, we know it.

JOHANN WOLFGANG VON GOETHE

If we don't have a hidden life with God,
our public life for God cannot bear fruit.

HENRI J. M. NOUWEN

✛ ✛ ✛

*Oh, the joys of those who do not follow
the advice of the wicked, or stand around
with sinners, or join in with mockers.
But they delight in the law of the LORD;
meditating on it day and night. They are like
trees planted along the riverbank, bearing
fruit each season. Their leaves never wither,
and they prosper in all they do.*

PSALM 1:1–3 NLT

Love is a fruit in season at all times,
and within the reach of every hand.

MOTHER TERESA

Friendship with God

Friendship with God is a two-way street....
Jesus said that He tells His friends all that His
Father has told Him; close friends communicate
thoroughly and make a transfer of heart and
thought. How awesome is our opportunity to be
friends with God, the almighty Creator of all!

BEVERLY LaHAYE

Have you noticed my friend Job? There's no one
quite like him—honest and true to his word,
totally devoted to God and hating evil.

JOB 1:8 MSG

God's friendship is the unexpected joy we
find when we reach His outstretched hand.

JANET L. SMITH

Steep yourself in God-reality, God-initiative, God-provisions.... You're my dearest friends! The Father wants to give you the very kingdom itself.

LUKE 12:28 MSG

✛ ✛ ✛

*I have called you friends,
for all things that I have heard from
My Father I have made known to you.*

JOHN 15:15 NASB

We can look to God as our Father. We can have a personal sense of His love for us and His interest in us, for He is concerned about us as a father is concerned for his children.... Incredible as it may seem, God wants our companionship. He wants to have us close to Him. He wants to be a father to us, to shield us, to protect us, to counsel us, and to guide us in our way through life.

BILLY GRAHAM

Greater Love

Clothe yourselves with compassion,
kindness, humility, gentleness and patience.
Bear with each other and forgive whatever
grievances you may have against one another.
Forgive as the Lord forgave you. And over
all these virtues put on love, which binds
them all together in perfect unity.

COLOSSIANS 3:12–14 NIV

Love must be sincere....
Honor one another above yourselves.

ROMANS 12:9–10 NIV

You are God's gift to each other
for the living of these days.

RANDY BECTON

Serve one another in love. For the whole
law can be summed up in this one command:
"Love your neighbor as yourself."

GALATIANS 5:13–14 NLT

What reveals a genuine love for God
is my ability to convince my family
and others of my love for them.

JACK FROST

✛ ✛ ✛

*This is My commandment, that you
love one another, just as I have loved you.
Greater love has no one than this,
that one lay down his life for his friends.*

JOHN 15:12–13 NASB

In God's wisdom, He frequently chooses
to meet our needs by showing His love toward
us through the hands and hearts of others.

JACK HAYFORD

Be kind and compassionate to
one another, forgiving each other,
just as in Christ God forgave you.

EPHESIANS 4:32 NIV

God's Care

The LORD is my shepherd; I shall not want.
He maketh me to lie down in green pastures:
he leadeth me beside the still waters. He
restoreth my soul: he leadeth me in the paths
of righteousness for his name's sake. Yea, though
I walk through the valley of the shadow of
death, I will fear no evil: for thou art with me;
thy rod and thy staff they comfort me. Thou
preparest a table before me in the presence of
mine enemies: thou anointest my head with
oil; my cup runneth over. Surely goodness and
mercy shall follow me all the days of my life: and
I will dwell in the house of the LORD for ever.

PSALM 23:1–6 KJV

God never abandons anyone on whom He has
set His love; nor does Christ, the good shepherd,
ever lose track of His sheep.

J. I. PACKER

✢ ✢ ✢

If God cares so wonderfully for
wildflowers that are here today
and thrown into the fire tomorrow,
he will certainly care for you.

MATTHEW 6:30 NLT

God cares for the world He created,
from the rising of a nation to the falling
of the sparrow. Everything in the world
lies under the watchful gaze of His
providential eyes, from the numbering
of the days of our life to the numbering
of the hairs on our head. When we look
at the world from that perspective,
it produces within us a response of reverence.

KEN GIRE

Divine Romance

Get into the habit of saying, "Speak, Lord,"
and life will become a romance.

OSWALD CHAMBERS

✠ ✠ ✠

*To fall in love with God is the
greatest of all romances—to seek Him
the greatest of all adventures, to find
Him the greatest human achievement.*

AUGUSTINE

Nothing in all creation will ever be able
to separate us from the love of God.

ROMANS 8:39 NLT

God's love is like a river springing up
in the Divine Substance and flowing
endlessly through His creation, filling all
things with life and goodness and strength.

THOMAS MERTON

He brought me to the banqueting house,
and his banner over me was love.

SONG OF SOLOMON 2:4 KJV

Love Him totally who gave
Himself totally for your love.

CLARE OF ASSISI

We know how much God loves us, and we have
put our trust in his love. God is love, and all who
live in love live in God, and God lives in them.

1 JOHN 4:16 NLT

God's holy beauty comes near you, like a spiritual
scent, and it stirs your drowsing soul....
He creates in you the desire to find Him
and run after Him—to follow wherever
He leads you, and to press peacefully against
His heart wherever He is. If you are seeking after
God, you may be sure of this: God is seeking you
much more. He is the Lover, and you are His
beloved. He has promised Himself to you.

JOHN OF THE CROSS

Immeasurable Love

We are so preciously loved by God
that we cannot even comprehend it.
No created being can ever know how much
and how sweetly and tenderly God loves them.
It is only with the help of His grace that
we are able to persevere in...endless wonder
at the high, surpassing, immeasurable love
which our Lord in His goodness has for us.

JULIAN OF NORWICH

Then Christ will make his home in your
hearts as you trust in him. Your roots will grow
down into God's love and keep you strong.

EPHESIANS 3:17 NLT

I have loved you with an everlasting love;
I have drawn you with loving-kindness.

JEREMIAH 31:3 NIV

If you have a special need today, focus your full attention on the goodness and greatness of your Father rather than on the size of your need. Your need is so small compared to His ability to meet it.

✝ ✝ ✝

God says, "I love you no matter what you do." His love is unconditional and unending.

Do not dwell upon your inner failings.… Just do this: Bring your soul to the Great Physician—exactly as you are, even and especially at your worst moment.… For it is in such moments that you will most readily sense His healing presence.

TERESA OF AVILA

Simple Faith

Now faith is being sure of what we hope for
and certain of what we do not see.... By faith
we understand that the universe was formed
at God's command, so that what is seen
was not made out of what was visible....
And without faith it is impossible
to please God, because anyone who comes
to him must believe that he exists and that
he rewards those who earnestly seek him.

HEBREWS 11:1, 3, 6 NIV

You are a child of your heavenly Father.
Confide in Him. Your faith in His love
and power can never be bold enough.

BASILEA SCHLINK

✟ ✟ ✟

The Lord said, "If you had faith like a mustard seed, you would say to this mulberry tree, 'Be uprooted and be planted in the sea'; and it would obey you."

LUKE 17:6 NASB

As the beloved of God
under the shadow
of His wings—
As a well-watered garden,
and as the apple of God's eye—
the seeds of great faith live within us.

Faith, as the Bible defines it, is present-tense
action. Faith means being sure of what we
hope for...now. It means knowing something is
real, this moment, all around you, even when you
don't see it. Great faith isn't the ability to believe
long and far into the misty future. It's simply
taking God at His word and taking the next step.

JONI EARECKSON TADA

Love Light

May God send His love like sunshine
in His warm and gentle way,
To fill each corner of your heart
each moment of today.

✢ ✢ ✢

*Your love, O Lord, reaches to the
heavens, your faithfulness to the skies....
For with you is the fountain of life;
in your light we see light.*

PSALM 36:5–9 NIV

From the world we see, hear, and touch, we
behold inspired visions that reveal God's glory.
In the sun's light, we catch warm rays of grace
and glimpse His eternal design. In the birds'
song, we hear His voice and it reawakens our
desire for Him. At the wind's touch, we feel His
Spirit and sense our eternal existence.

WENDY MOORE

God is the sunshine that warms us, the rain
that melts the frost and waters the young plants.
The presence of God is a climate of strong
and bracing love, always there.

JOAN ARNOLD

Lord, let the glow of Your love
Through my whole being shine
Fill me with gladness from above
and hold me by strength Divine
Lord, make Your Light in my Heart
Glow radiant and clear, never to part.

MARGARET FISHBACK POWERS

In the same way, let your good deeds
shine out for all to see, so that everyone
will praise your heavenly Father.

MATTHEW 5:16 NLT

The fountain of beauty is the heart,
and every generous thought illustrates
the walls of your chamber.

FRANCIS QUARLES

The Palm of His Hand

The mystery of life is that the Lord of life
cannot be known except in and through
the act of living. Without the concrete
and specific involvements of daily life we
cannot come to know the loving presence
of Him who holds us in the palm of His
hand.... Therefore, we are called each day to
present to our Lord the whole of our lives.

HENRI J. M. NOUWEN

I'm a little pencil in the hands of a loving
God who is writing a love letter to the world.

MOTHER TERESA

✝ ✝ ✝

The LORD directs the steps of the godly.
He delights in every detail of their lives.
Though they stumble, they will never fall,
for the LORD holds them by the hand.

PSALM 37:23–24 NLT

God promises to keep us in the palm of His hand, with or without our awareness. God has already made a space for us, even if we have not made a space for God.

DAVID AND BARBARA SORENSEN

The God who holds the whole world in His hands wraps Himself in the splendor of the sun's light and walks among the clouds.

That Hand which bears all nature up
Shall guard His children well.

WILLIAM COWPER

Behold, I have inscribed you
on the palms of My hands.

ISAIAH 49:16 NASB

The Love of God

Your roots will grow down into God's love
and keep you strong. And may you have
the power to understand, as all God's people
should, how wide, how long, how high,
and how deep his love really is.

EPHESIANS 3:17–18 NLT

The heart is rich when it is content,
and it is always content when its desires are fixed
on God. Nothing can bring greater happiness
than doing God's will for the love of God.

MIGUEL FEBRES CORDERO-MUÑOZ

✦ ✦ ✦

*Be perfect, be of good comfort,
be of one mind, live in peace; and the God
of love and peace shall be with you.*

2 CORINTHIANS 13:11 KJV

The love of God is broader than the measure
of our mind
And the heart of the Eternal is most
wonderfully kind.

FREDERICK W. FABER

Who shall separate us from the love of Christ?
Shall trouble or hardship or persecution or
famine or nakedness or danger or sword?...
No, in all these things we are more than
conquerors through him who loved us. For
I am convinced that neither death nor life,
neither angels nor demons, neither the present
nor the future, nor any powers, neither height
nor depth, nor anything else in all creation,
will be able to separate us from the love of
God that is in Christ Jesus our Lord.

ROMANS 8:35–39 NIV

Wonder and Praise

If you have never heard the mountains singing,
or seen the trees of the field clapping their hands,
do not think because of that they don't. Ask
God to open your ears so you may hear it, and
your eyes so you may see it, because, though few
people ever know it, they do, my friend, they do.

PHILLIPS MCCANDLISH

The LORD is my strength and my song;
he has become my salvation.
He is my God, and I will praise him,
my father's God, and I will exalt him....
Who is like you—majestic in holiness,
awesome in glory, working wonders?

EXODUS 15:2, 11 NIV

The wonder of living is held within the
beauty of silence, the glory of sunlight...
the sweetness of fresh spring air, the
quiet strength of earth, and the love that
lies at the very root of all things.

✠ ✠ ✠

*Who can list the glorious
miracles of the LORD? Who can
ever praise him enough?*

PSALM 106:2 NLT

The love of the Father is like
a sudden rain shower that will
pour forth when you least expect it,
catching you up into wonder and praise.

RICHARD J. FOSTER

Surrounded

The light of God surrounds me,
The love of God enfolds me,
The presence of God watches over me,
Wherever I am, God is.

✛ ✛ ✛

O Lord, you bless the righteous;
you surround them with
your favor as with a shield.

PSALM 5:12 NIV

The Lord's goodness surrounds us at every
moment. I walk through it almost with
difficulty, as through thick grass and flowers.

R. W. Barber

What can harm us when everything must first
touch God whose presence surrounds us?

He surrounds them continuously
and preserves them from every harm.

DEUTERONOMY 33:12 NLT

I tread no path in life to Him unknown;
I lift no burden, bear no pain, alone;
my soul a calm, sure hiding place has found;
the everlasting arms my life surround.

ROBERT BROWNING

Stay in the secret place till the surrounding
noises begin to fade out of your heart
and a sense of God's presence envelops you....
Listen for the inward Voice till you learn to
recognize it. Stop trying to compete with others.
Give yourself to God and then be what and who
you are without regard to what others think.

A. W. TOZER

Walking in His Ways

God's love, though, is ever and always,
eternally present to all who fear him,
making everything right for them and their
children as they follow his Covenant ways
and remember to do whatever he said.

PSALM 103:17–18 MSG

Without the Way, there is no going;
without the Truth, there is no knowing;
without the Life, there is no living.

THOMAS À KEMPIS

If you are pleased with me,
teach me your ways so I may know you
and continue to find favor with you.

EXODUS 33:13 NIV

Be simple; take our Lord's
hand and walk through things.

FATHER ANDREW

✝ ✝ ✝

*Love God, your God. Walk in his
ways. Keep his commandments,
regulations, and rules so that you
will live, really live, live exuberantly,
blessed by God.... Love God,
your God, listening obediently
to him, firmly embracing him.
Oh yes, he is life itself.*

DEUTERONOMY 30:16, 20 MSG

Be assured, if you walk with Him and
look to Him and expect help from Him,
He will never fail you.

GEORGE MÜLLER

Yes, LORD, walking in the way
of your laws, we wait for you;
your name and renown are
the desire of our hearts.

ISAIAH 26:8 NIV

Love Always

God loves us for ourselves.
He values our love more than He values
galaxies of new created worlds.

A. W. TOZER

If you believe in God, it is not too difficult
to believe that He is concerned about the
universe and all the events on this earth. But
the really staggering message of the Bible is
that this same God cares deeply about you
and your identity and the events of your
life.... We have missed the full impact of the
Gospel if we have not discovered what it is
to be ourselves, loved by God, irreplaceable
in His sight, unique among our fellowmen.

BRUCE LARSON

I'll never quit telling the story of your love....
Your love has always been our lives' foundation,
your fidelity has been the roof over our world.

PSALM 89:2 MSG

Our greatness rests solely on the fact that God in
His incomprehensible goodness has bestowed His
love upon us. God does not love us because we are
so valuable; we are valuable because God loves us.

HELMUT THIELICKE

✟ ✟ ✟

*For GOD is sheer beauty, all-generous
in love, loyal always and ever.*

PSALM 100:5 MSG

Let your faith in Christ, the omnipresent One, be
in the quiet confidence that He will every day and
every moment keep you as the apple of His eye.

ANDREW MURRAY

My Help

I will lift up my eyes to the mountains;
from where shall my help come? My help comes
from the LORD, who made heaven and earth.
He will not allow your foot to slip; He who
keeps you will not slumber. Behold, He who
keeps Israel will neither slumber nor sleep. The
LORD is your keeper; the LORD is your shade
on your right hand. The sun will not smite you
by day, nor the moon by night. The LORD will
protect you from all evil; He will keep your soul.
The LORD will guard your going out and your
coming in from this time forth and forever.

PSALM 121:1–8 NASB

Whatever God tells us to do,
He also helps us to do.

DORA GREENWELL

We have a Father in heaven who
is almighty, who loves His children as He
loves His only-begotten Son, and whose
very joy and delight it is to...help them
at all times and under all circumstances.

GEORGE MÜLLER

✝ ✝ ✝

*God's strong name is our help,
the same God who made
heaven and earth.*

PSALM 124:8 MSG

When we pray we should keep in mind all
of the shortcomings and excesses we feel,
and pour them out freely to God,
our faithful Father, who is ready to help.

MARTIN LUTHER

Nothing but Grace

God is able to make all grace abound to you, so
that in all things at all times, having all that you
need, you will abound in every good work.

2 CORINTHIANS 9:8 NIV

Grace is no stationary thing, it is ever becoming.
It is flowing straight out of God's heart.
Grace does nothing but reform and convey God.
Grace makes the soul conformable
to the will of God. God, the ground
of the soul, and grace go together.

JOHANNES ECKHART

✦ ✦ ✦

*Grace and gratitude belong together
like heaven and earth. Grace evokes
gratitude like the voice an echo. Gratitude
follows grace as thunder follows lightning.*

KARL BARTH

God is sheer mercy and grace; not easily
angered, he's rich in love.... As far as sunrise is
from sunset, he has separated us from our sins.

PSALM 103:8, 12 MSG

To be grateful is to recognize the love of God
in everything He has given us—and He
has given us everything. Every breath
we draw is a gift of His love, every moment
of existence is a gift of grace.

THOMAS MERTON

God did it for us. Out of sheer generosity he
put us in right standing with himself. A pure
gift. He got us out of the mess we're in and
restored us to where he always wanted us to be.
And he did it by means of Jesus Christ.

ROMANS 3:23–24 MSG

Showers of Blessings

Bless the LORD, O my soul; and all that
is within me, bless His holy name! Bless the
LORD, O my soul, and forget not all His
benefits: who forgives all your iniquities, who
heals all your diseases, who redeems your
life from destruction, who crowns you with
lovingkindness and tender mercies, who satisfies
your mouth with good things, so that your
youth is renewed like the eagle's.

PSALM 103:1–5 NKJV

✝ ✝ ✝

*I will send the showers they need.
There will be showers of blessings.*

EZEKIEL 34:26 NLT

God, who is love—who is, if I may say it this
way, made out of love—simply cannot help but
shed blessing on blessing upon us.

HANNAH WHITALL SMITH

All perfect gifts are from above and all our
blessings show
The amplitude of God's dear love which
any heart may know.

LAURA LEE RANDALL

From the fullness of his grace we have
all received one blessing after another.

JOHN 1:16 NIV

There is plentitude in God....
God is a vast reservoir of blessing
who supplies us abundantly.

EUGENE PETERSON

However many blessings we expect
from God, His infinite liberality will always
exceed all our wishes and our thoughts.

JOHN CALVIN

Totally Aware

God is every moment totally aware of
each one of us. Totally aware in intense
concentration and love.... No one passes
through any area of life, happy or tragic,
without the attention of God with them.

EUGENIA PRICE

GOD takes care of all who stay close to him

PSALM 31:23 MSG

Because God is responsible for our welfare,
we are told to cast all our care upon Him,
for He cares for us. God says, "I'll take the
burden—don't give it a thought—leave it
to Me." God is keenly aware that we are
dependent upon Him for life's necessities.

BILLY GRAHAM

I lay down and slept,
yet I woke up in safety,
for the LORD was watching over me.

PSALM 3:5 NLT

You are God's created beauty
and the focus of His affection and delight.

JANET L. SMITH

Live carefree before God;
he is most careful with you.

1 PETER 5:7 MSG

✜ ✜ ✜

*From the tiny birds of the air and from
the fragile lilies of the field we learn
the same truth, which is so important for
those who desire a life of simple faith:
God takes care of His own. He knows
our needs. He anticipates our crises.*

CHARLES SWINDOLL

Sing Praise

All enjoyment spontaneously overflows into praise.... The world rings with praise...walkers praising the countryside, players praising their favorite game.... I think we delight to praise what we enjoy because the praise not merely expresses but completes the enjoyment; it is the appointed consummation.

C. S. LEWIS

Earth, with her thousand voices, praises God.

SAMUEL TAYLOR COLERIDGE

God's pursuit of praise from us and our pursuit of pleasure in Him are one and the same pursuit. God's quest to be glorified and our quest to be satisfied reach their goal in this one experience: our delight in God which overflows in praise.

JOHN PIPER

✠ ✠ ✠

O sing unto the LORD a new song:
sing unto the LORD, all the earth.

PSALM 96:1 KJV

Praise ye the LORD. Praise God in his sanctuary:
praise him in the firmament of his power.
Praise him for his mighty acts: praise him
according to his excellent greatness. Praise him
with the sound of the trumpet: praise him
with the psaltery and harp. Praise him with the
timbrel and dance: praise him with stringed
instruments and organs. Praise him upon
the loud cymbals: praise him upon the high
sounding cymbals. Let every thing that hath
breath praise the LORD. Praise ye the LORD.

PSALM 150:1–6 KJV

Love Never Fails

If I speak with the tongues of men and of angels, but do not have love, I have become a noisy gong or a clanging cymbal. If I have the gift of prophecy, and know all mysteries and all knowledge; and if I have all faith, so as to remove mountains, but do not have love, I am nothing. And if I give all my possessions to feed the poor, and if I surrender my body to be burned, but do not have love, it profits me nothing. Love is patient, love is kind and is not jealous; love does not brag and is not arrogant, does not act unbecomingly; it does not seek its own, is not provoked, does not take into account a wrong suffered, does not rejoice in unrighteousness, but rejoices with the truth; bears all things, believes all things, hopes all things, endures all things. Love never fails.

1 CORINTHIANS 13:1–8 NASB

An instant of pure love is more precious to God...
than all other good works together.

JOHN OF THE CROSS

✝ ✝ ✝

*Show us your unfailing love, O Lord,
and grant us your salvation.*

PSALM 85:7 NIV

The King of love my Shepherd is,
Whose goodness faileth never;
I nothing lack if I am His,
And He is mine forever.

SIR HENRY WILLIAMS BAKER

[God's] heart is the most sensitive
and tender of all. No act goes unnoticed,
no matter how insignificant or small.

RICHARD J. FOSTER

The Garden of His Love

It is God's knowledge of me, His careful
husbanding of the ground of my being,
His constant presence in the garden
of my little life that guarantees my joy.

W. PHILLIP KELLER

It's only a tiny rosebud—
A flower of God's design;
But I cannot unfold the petals
With these clumsy hands of mine.
And the pathway that lies before me
Only my Heavenly Father knows—
I'll trust Him to unfold the moments
Just as He unfolds the rose.

✤ ✤ ✤

*God made you grow. It's not the one
who plants or the one who waters who
is at the center of this process but God,
who makes things grow.*

1 CORINTHIANS 3:6 MSG

A wise gardener plants his seeds,
then has the good sense not to dig
them up every few days to see if a
crop is on the way. Likewise,
we must be patient as God brings
the answers...in His own good time.

QUIN SHERRER

Ah, Sovereign LORD, you have made
the heavens and the earth by your
great power and outstretched arm.
Nothing is too hard for you.

JEREMIAH 32:17 NIV

At heart, the symbolism
of the garden relates back to Eden,
where the wonder and joy of God's
creation was new and fresh and untainted.

PHILIP GLASSBOROW

His Imprint

Each of us, made in His image
and likeness, is yet another promise
He has made to the universe that He
will continue to love it and care for it.

BRENNAN MANNING

So God created man in his own image,
in the image of God he created him;
male and female he created them.

GENESIS 1:27 NIV

In the very beginning it was God who
formed us by His Word. He made us in His
own image. God was spirit and He gave us
a spirit so that He could come into us and
mingle His own life with our life.

MADAME JEANNE GUYON

Made in His image, we can have real meaning,
and we can have real knowledge through
what He has communicated to us.

FRANCIS SCHAEFFER

For in Him all the fullness of Deity
dwells in bodily form, and in Him you
have been made complete.

COLOSSIANS 2:9–10 NASB

✝ ✝ ✝

*The God of the universe—the One who
created everything and holds it all in His
hand—created each of us in His image,
to bear His likeness, His imprint. It is
only when Christ dwells within our hearts,
radiating the pure light of His love through
our humanity, that we discover who we are
and what we were intended to be.*

Every single act of love bears the imprint of God.

Fear Not

Don't be afraid, I've redeemed you. I've called
your name. You're mine. When you're in over
your head, I'll be there with you. When you're
in rough waters, you will not go down.
When you're between a rock and a hard place,
it won't be a dead end—Because I am God,
your personal God, The Holy of Israel,
your Savior. I paid a huge price for you...!
That's how much you mean to me!
That's how much I love you!

ISAIAH 43:1–4 MSG

Do not be afraid to enter the cloud that
is settling down on your life. God is in it.
The other side is radiant with His glory.

L. B. COWMAN

If God be for us, who can be against us?

ROMANS 8:31 KJV

What have we to expect? Anything.
What have we to hope for? Everything.
What have we to fear? Nothing.

EDWARD B. PUSEY

✠ ✠ ✠

*Be strong and of good courage, do not
fear nor be afraid of them; for the LORD
your God, He is the One who goes with you.
He will not leave you nor forsake you.*

DEUTERONOMY 31:6 NKJV

[God] comforts. He lays His right hand
on the soul wounded by weariness, or fear,
or any kind of weakness at all. And He says,
as if that one were the only soul in all the universe:
O...greatly beloved, fear not: peace be unto you.
Be strong—yea, be strong!

AMY CARMICHAEL

At Home in His Love

Make your home in me just as I do in you. In
the same way that a branch can't bear grapes
by itself but only by being joined to the vine,
you can't bear fruit unless you are joined with
me. I am the Vine, you are the branches.
When you're joined with me and I with you,
the relation intimate and organic, the harvest
is sure to be abundant. Separated, you can't
produce a thing.... But if you make yourselves
at home with me and my words are at home
in you, you can be sure that whatever you
ask will be listened to and acted upon.... I've
loved you the way my Father has loved me.
Make yourselves at home in my love.

JOHN 15:4–9 MSG

✝ ✝ ✝

*God is always present in the temple
of your heart...His home. And when you
come in to meet Him there, you find that
it is the one place of deep satisfaction
where every longing is met.*

This is and has been the Father's
work from the beginning—to bring
us into the home of His heart.

GEORGE MACDONALD

How lovely are Your dwelling places, O LORD
of hosts! My soul longed and even yearned
for the courts of the LORD; my heart and my
flesh sing for joy to the living God.... For a day
in Your courts is better than a thousand outside.

Psalm 84:1–2, 10 nasb

An Undivided Heart

Above all else, guard your heart,
for it is the wellspring of life.

PROVERBS 4:23 NIV

In comparison with this big world,
the human heart is only a small thing.
Though the world is so large, it is utterly
unable to satisfy this tiny heart. Our ever
growing soul and its capacities can be
satisfied only in the infinite God.

SADHU SUNDAR SINGH

"Love the Lord your God with all
your heart and with all your soul
and with all your mind." This is the first
and greatest commandment.

MATTHEW 22:37–38 NIV

✜ ✜ ✜

*I will give them an undivided heart
and put a new spirit in them; I will remove
from them their heart of stone and give
them a heart of flesh. Then they will follow
my decrees...they will be my people,
and I will be their God.*

EZEKIEL 11:19–20 NIV

Whom have I in heaven but You?
And besides You, I desire nothing on earth.
My flesh and my heart may fail, but God is the
strength of my heart and my portion forever.

PSALM 73:25–26 NASB

Open wide the windows of our spirits
and fill us full of light; open wide the door
of our hearts, that we may receive and entertain
Thee with all our powers of adoration.

CHRISTINA ROSSETTI

Faithful Guide

God, who has led you safely on so far,
will lead you on to the end. Be altogether
at rest in the loving holy confidence which you
ought to have in His heavenly Providence.

FRANCIS DE SALES

The LORD will guide you always;
he will satisfy your needs in a sun-scorched
land…. You will be like a well-watered garden,
like a spring whose waters never fail.

ISAIAH 58:11 NIV

Heaven often seems distant and unknown,
but if he who made the road…is our guide,
we need not fear to lose the way.

HENRY VAN DYKE

The love that keeps us through the passing
night will guide us and keep us still.

✢ ✢ ✢

*The Lord leads with unfailing love and
faithfulness all who keep his covenant.*

PSALM 25:10 NLT

Guidance is a sovereign act. Not merely does God
will to guide us by showing us His way...whatever
mistakes we may make, we shall come safely home.
Slippings and strayings there will be, no doubt,
but the everlasting arms are beneath us; we shall be
caught, rescued, restored. This is God's promise;
this is how good He is. And our self-distrust, while
keeping us humble, must not cloud the joy with
which we lean on our faithful covenant God.

J. I. PACKER

Indescribable Love

Could we with ink the ocean fill,
And were the skies of parchment made,
Were every stalk on earth a quill,
And every man a scribe by trade
To write the love of God above
Would drain the ocean dry,
Nor could the scroll contain the whole
Though stretched from sky to sky.

MEIR BEN ISAAC NEHORAI

✦ ✦ ✦

*God defines love not as a mere
human sentiment but a divine
desire for our well-being.*

ROSE GOBLE

I pray that your love will overflow more
and more, and that you will keep on growing
in knowledge and understanding.

PHILIPPIANS 1:9 NLT

Love is the response of the heart to the overwhelming goodness of God.... You may be so awestruck and full of love at His presence that words do not come.

RICHARD J. FOSTER

Watch what God does, and then you do it, like children who learn proper behavior from their parents. Mostly what God does is love you. Keep company with him and learn a life of love. Observe how Christ loved us. His love was not cautious but extravagant. He didn't love in order to get something from us but to give everything of himself to us. Love like that.

EPHESIANS 5:1–2 MSG

Every Need

God wants nothing from us except our needs,
and these furnish Him with room to display His
bounty when He supplies them freely.... Not
what I have, but what I do not have, is the first
point of contact between my soul and God.

CHARLES H. SPURGEON

Jesus Christ has brought every need,
every joy, every gratitude, every hope
of ours before God. He accompanies us
and brings us into the presence of God.

DIETRICH BONHOEFFER

Be still, and in the quiet moments listen
to the voice of your Heavenly Father.
His words can renew your spirit. No one knows
you and your needs like He does.

JANET L. SMITH

✛ ✛ ✛

*My God shall supply all
your need according to his riches
in glory by Christ Jesus.*

PHILIPPIANS 4:19 KJV

The "air" which our souls need also
envelops all of us at all times and on all sides.
God is round about us...on every hand,
with many-sided and all-sufficient grace.

OLE HALLESBY

Where there is faith, there is love.
Where there is love, there is peace.
Where there is peace, there is God.
Where there is God, there is no need.

Good Gifts

He has not left himself without testimony:
He has shown kindness by giving you rain
from heaven and crops in their seasons;
he provides you with plenty of food
and fills your hearts with joy.

ACTS 14:17–18 NIV

Give generously, for your gifts
will return to you later.

ECCLESIASTES 11:1 NLT

The impetus of God's love comes from within
Himself, to share with us His life and love. It
is a beautiful, eternal gift, held out to us in the
hands of love. All we have to do is say "Yes!"

JOHN POWELL, S.J.

✛ ✛ ✛

*Every good gift and every perfect gift
is from above, and cometh down from
the Father of lights, with whom is no
variableness, neither shadow of turning.*

JAMES 1:17 KJV

Rejoice in the LORD your God!
For the rains he sends demonstrates his
faithfulness. Once more the autumn rains
will come, as well as the rains of spring.

JOEL 2:23 NLT

God has a wonderful plan for each person
He has chosen. He knew even before
He created this world what beauty He would
bring forth from our lives.

LOUIS B. WYLY

Enfolded in Peace

I will let God's peace infuse every part of today.
As the chaos swirls and life's demands pull
at me on all sides, I will breathe in God's
peace that surpasses all understanding.
He has promised that He would set within
me a peace too deeply planted to be affected
by unexpected or exhausting demands.

WENDY MOORE

Because of the tender mercy of our God,
with which the Sunrise from on high will visit
us, to shine upon those who sit in darkness…
to guide our feet into the way of peace.

LUKE 1:78–79 NASB

God cannot give us a happiness and peace
apart from Himself, because it is not there.
There is no such thing.

C. S. LEWIS

Calm me, O Lord, as you stilled the storm,
Still me, O Lord, keep me from harm.
Let all the tumult within me cease,
Enfold me, Lord, in your peace.

CELTIC TRADITIONAL

✠ ✠ ✠

*In His love He clothes us, enfolds us,
and embraces us; that tender love
completely surrounds us, never to leave us.*

JULIAN OF NORWICH

The peace of God, which transcends
all understanding, will guard your hearts
and your minds in Christ Jesus.

PHILIPPIANS 4:7 NIV

God Is Our Refuge

Hear my cry, O God; Give heed to my prayer. From the end of the earth I call to You when my heart is faint; lead me to the rock that is higher than I. For You have been a refuge for me, a tower of strength against the enemy. Let me dwell in Your tent forever; let me take refuge in the shelter of Your wings.

PSALM 61:1–4 NASB

When God has become...our refuge and our fortress, then we can reach out to Him in the midst of a broken world and feel at home while still on the way.

HENRI J. M. NOUWEN

✣ ✣ ✣

*Whom have I in heaven but You?
And besides You, I desire nothing on
earth. My flesh and my heart may fail,
but God is the strength of my heart
and my portion forever.... As for me,
the nearness of God is my good;
I have made the Lord God my refuge.*

PSALM 73:25–26, 28 NASB

Our Savior pictures Himself not merely as the Rock of Ages, and our Strong Rock of Refuge, but the Rock of our Salvation. Here, in Him and upon His merit and atoning grace, we were saved from among the lost. Let us glory in this precious name and never forget that He was "wounded for our transgressions" and "that he bore our sins in his own body on the tree."

CHARLES E. HURLBURT AND T. C. HORTON

Shepherd of Love

The King of love my Shepherd is,
Whose goodness faileth never;
I nothing lack if I am His,
And He is mine forever.

SIR HENRY WILLIAMS BAKER

He calls his own sheep by name
and leads them out.... His sheep follow
him because they know his voice.

JOHN 10:3–4 NIV

God is the shepherd in search of His lamb.
His legs are scratched, His feet are sore and
His eyes are burning. He scales the cliffs and
traverses the fields. He explores the caves.
He cups His hands to His mouth and calls into
the canyon. And the name He calls is yours.

MAX LUCADO

Abandon yourself to His care and guidance,
as a sheep in the care of a shepherd,
and trust Him utterly.

HANNAH WHITALL SMITH

Is any name more comforting to weary,
needy children of our God than Jesus' name
of Shepherd? Feeding, leading beside
still water, watching over all our wanderings,
bringing us…out of the wilderness over
the Jordan into the land of peace and plenty.

CHARLES E. HURLBURT AND T. C. HORTON

✢ ✢ ✢

*I am the good shepherd; I know my
sheep and my sheep know me—just as
the Father knows me and I know the
Father—and I lay down my life for the sheep.*

JOHN 10:14–15 NIV

New Creation

For Christ's love compels us, because we
are convinced that one died for all,
and therefore all died. And he died for all,
that those who live should no longer
live for themselves but for him who died for
them and was raised again.... Therefore,
if anyone is in Christ, he is a new creation.

2 Corinthians 5:14–15, 17 NIV

When God's power touches a mere human
being, something happens! Creation all
over again! The life-changing touch of love!

Gloria Gaither

Forget the former things; do not dwell
on the past. See, I am doing a new thing!

Isaiah 43:18–19 NIV

You are a little less than angels,
crown of creation, image of God.
Each person is a revelation,
a transfiguration, a waiting
for Him to manifest Himself.

EDWARD FARRELL

✣ ✣ ✣

*Let the Spirit renew your thoughts and
attitudes. Put on your new nature, created
to be like God—truly righteous and holy.*

EPHESIANS 4:23–24 NLT

The Holy Spirit alone can change the heart.
[We] must be born again. Christ has said it.
It is not a change of sentiment, nor an outward
reformation of life; it is a new
heart implanted by the Holy Spirit.

MARY WINSLOW

God's Beautiful Peace

As water is restless until it reaches its level,
so the soul has no peace until it rests in God.

SADHU SUNDAR SINGH

✝ ✝ ✝

*Peace is a margin of power around
our daily need. Peace is a consciousness
of springs too deep for earthly
droughts to dry up.*

HARRY EMERSON FOSDICK

Drop Thy still dews of quietness
till all our strivings cease;
take from our souls the strain and stress,
and let our ordered lives confess
the beauty of Thy peace.

JOHN GREENLEAF WHITTIER

Be still, and know that I am God.

PSALM 46:10 KJV

For me, the idea that God Himself suffered
was always one of the most convincing
teachings of Christianity. I think that God
is closer to suffering than to happiness,
and to find God in this manner gives peace
and rest, and a strong and courageous heart.

DIETRICH BONHOEFFER

The LORD bless you and keep you;
The LORD make His face shine upon you,
And be gracious to you;
The LORD lift up His countenance upon you,
And give you peace.

NUMBERS 6:24–26 NKJV

Source of Wonder

Dear Lord, grant me the grace of wonder.
Surprise me, amaze me, awe me in every
crevice of your universe.... Each day enrapture
me with your marvelous things without number.
I do not ask to see the reason for it all;
I ask only to share the wonder of it all.

JOSHUA ABRAHAM HESCHEL

May our lives be illumined
by the steady radiance
renewed daily,
of a wonder,
the source of which
is beyond reason.

DAG HAMMARSKJÖLD

I would maintain that thanks are
the highest form of thought, and that gratitude
is happiness doubled by wonder.

G. K. CHESTERTON

✝ ✝ ✝

*I will give thanks to the LORD with all
my heart; I will tell of all Your wonders.
I will be glad and exult in You; I will sing
praise to Your name, O Most High.*

PSALM 9:1–2 NASB

As we grow in our capacities to see and
enjoy the joys that God has placed in our lives,
life becomes a glorious experience
of discovering His endless wonders.

Show the wonder of your great love,
you who save by your right hand
those who take refuge in you from their foes.
Keep me as the apple of your eye;
hide me in the shadow of your wings

PSALM 17:7–8 NIV

New Every Morning

Always new. Always exciting.
Always full of promise. The mornings
of our lives, each a personal daily miracle!

GLORIA GAITHER

That is God's call to us—simply to be
people who are content to live close to Him
and to renew the kind of life in which
the closeness is felt and experienced.

THOMAS MERTON

Weeping may remain for a night,
but rejoicing comes in the morning.

PSALM 30:5 NIV

For new, and new, and ever new,
The golden bud within the blue;
And every morning seems to say:
"There's something happy on the way."

HENRY VAN DYKE

A quiet morning with a loving God
puts the events of the upcoming day
into proper perspective.

JANETTE OKE

Life begins each morning.... Each morning
is the open door to a new world—new vistas,
new aims, new tryings.

LEIGH MITCHELL HODGES

✢ ✢ ✢

The LORD's lovingkindnesses indeed
never cease,
For His compassions never fail.
They are new every morning;
Great is Your faithfulness.

LAMENTATIONS 3:22–23 NASB

Don't get so busy that you miss the beauty of a day
or the serenity of a quiet moment alone. For it is
often life's smallest pleasures and gentlest joys that
make the biggest and most lasting difference.

A Life of Prayer

They who seek the throne of grace find that
throne in every place;
If we live a life of prayer,
God is present everywhere.

OLIVER HOLDEN

Do not be anxious about anything, but in
everything, by prayer and petition, with
thanksgiving, present your requests to God.

PHILIPPIANS 4:6 NIV

Lord...give me the gift of faith to be
renewed and shared with others each day.
Teach me to live this moment only,
looking neither to the past with regret,
nor the future with apprehension.
Let love be my aim and my life a prayer.

ROSEANN ALEXANDER-ISHAM

Be joyful in hope, patient in affliction,
faithful in prayer.

ROMANS 12:12 NIV

Prayer is...an ever available door
by which to come into God's presence.

DOUGLAS V. STEERE

✛ ✛ ✛

*Our Father which art in heaven, hallowed
be thy name. Thy kingdom come. Thy will
be done in earth, as it is in heaven. Give us
this day our daily bread. And forgive us
our debts, as we forgive our debtors. And
lead us not into temptation, but deliver us
from evil: for thine is the kingdom, and the
power, and the glory, for ever. Amen.*

MATTHEW 6:9–13 KJV

Gratitude for Daily Graces

Thank you, God, for little things
That often come our way,
The things we take for granted
But don't mention when we pray.

The unexpected courtesy,
The thoughtful kindly deed,
A hand reached out to help us
In the time of sudden need.

Oh, make us more aware, dear God,
Of little daily graces
That come to us with sweet surprise
From never-dreamed-of places.

✤ ✤ ✤

Praise be to the Lord, to God our Savior,
who daily bears our burdens.

PSALM 68:19 NIV

Gratitude...takes nothing for granted,
is never unresponsive, is constantly
awakening to new wonder and to praise
of the goodness of God.

Thomas Merton

Even though on the outside it often looks
like things are falling apart on us, on the
inside, where God is making new life, not
a day goes by without his unfolding grace.

2 Corinthians 4:16 msg

Day-to-day living becomes a window
through which we get a glimpse
of life eternal. The eternal illuminates
and gives focus to the daily.

Janice Riggle Huie

Know the Lord

In our unquenchable longing to know God
personally, we pursue Him with passion and
find He is relentless in His pursuit of us.

"Let him who boasts boast of this, that he
understands and knows Me, that I am the
LORD who exercises lovingkindness, justice and
righteousness on earth; for I delight in these
things," declares the LORD.

JEREMIAH 9:24 NASB

What makes life worthwhile is having a big
enough objective, something which catches our
imagination and lays hold of our allegiance....
What higher, more exalted, and more
compelling goal can there be than to know God?

J. I. PACKER

✝ ✝ ✝

*I will be faithful to you and make
you mine, and you will finally
know me as the Lord.*

HOSEA 2:20 NLT

So let us know, let us press on to know
the LORD. His going forth is as certain as the
dawn; and He will come to us like the rain,
like the spring rain watering the earth.

HOSEA 6:3 NASB

Joy comes from knowing God loves me
and knows who I am and where I'm going...that
my future is secure as I rest in Him.

JAMES DOBSON

In those times I can't seem to find God,
I rest in the assurance He knows how to find me.

NEVA COYLE

Love without Limits

Before anything else, above all else,
beyond everything else, God loves us.
God loves us extravagantly, ridiculously,
without limit or condition.
God is in love with us...God yearns for us.

ROBERTA BONDI

✢ ✢ ✢

*There is no limit to God's love.
It is without measure
and its depth cannot be sounded.*

MOTHER TERESA

Can you fathom the mysteries of God? Can
you probe the limits of the Almighty? They are
higher than the heavens—what can you do?
They are deeper than the depths of the grave—
what can you know? Their measure is longer
than the earth and wider than the sea.

JOB 11:7–9 NIV

Everything which relates to God is infinite.
We must therefore, while we keep our hearts
humble, keep our aims high. Our highest
services are indeed but finite, imperfect.
But as God is unlimited in goodness,
He should have our unlimited love.

HANNAH MORE

With God our trust can be abandoned,
utterly free. In Him are no limitations, no
flaws, no weaknesses. His judgment is perfect,
His knowledge of us is perfect, His love is
perfect. God alone is trustworthy.

EUGENIA PRICE

Let there be no limit to what we take
to God in prayer, so that there may be no
limit to God's reign and rule in all of life.

ROGER HAZELTON

God Is Enough

Nothing can separate you from His love,
absolutely nothing.... God is enough for time,
and God is enough for eternity. God is enough!

HANNAH WHITALL SMITH

My grace is enough; it's all you need. My
strength comes into its own in your weakness.

2 CORINTHIANS 12:9 MSG

✝ ✝ ✝

God, of Your goodness give
me Yourself, for You are enough for me.
And only in You do I have everything.

JULIAN OF NORWICH

He who has God and everything has
no more than he who has God alone.

C. S. LEWIS

Faith...has sustained me—faith in the God
of the Bible, a God, as someone once put it,
not small enough to be understood
but big enough to be worshipped.

ELISABETH ELLIOT

To know Him is to love Him and to know
Him better is to love Him more. We can get a
right start only by accepting God as He is and
learning to love Him for what He is. As we go
on to know Him better we shall find it a source
of unspeakable joy that God is just what He is....
O God, I have tasted Thy goodness, and it has
both satisfied me and made me thirsty for more.

A. W. TOZER

As the deer pants for streams of water,
so my soul pants for you, O God.
My soul thirsts for God, for the living God.

PSALM 42:1–2 NIV

Live in Harmony

The wisdom that comes from above is first of
all pure. It is also peace loving, gentle
at all times, and willing to yield to others.
It is full of mercy and good deeds. It shows
no favoritism and is always sincere.

JAMES 3:17 NLT

Drop Thy still dews of quietness
till all our strivings cease;
take from our souls the strain and stress,
and let our ordered lives confess
the beauty of Thy peace.

JOHN GREENLEAF WHITTIER

The highest excellence which an individual
can attain must be to work according
to the best of his genius and to work
in harmony with God's creation.

J. H. SMYTHE

Finally, all of you, live in harmony with one another; be sympathetic, love..., be compassionate and humble. Do not repay evil with evil or insult with insult, but with blessing, because to this you were called so that you may inherit a blessing.

1 PETER 3:8–9 NIV

✣ ✣ ✣

May God, who gives this patience and encouragement, help you live in complete harmony with each other.

ROMANS 15:5 NLT

To love other people means to see them as God intended them to be.

Love comes while we rest against our Father's chest.
Joy comes when we catch the rhythms of His heart.
Peace comes when we live in harmony with those rhythms.

KEN GIRE

God Listens

You can talk to God because God listens.
Your voice matters in heaven. He takes you
very seriously. When you enter His presence,
the attendants turn to you to hear your voice.
No need to fear that you will be ignored.
Even if you stammer or stumble,
even if what you have to say impresses no one,
it impresses God—and He listens.

MAX LUCADO

God listens in compassion and love,
just like we do when our children come to us.
He delights in our presence. When we
do this, we will discover something
of inestimable value. We will discover
that by praying we learn to pray.

RICHARD J. FOSTER

✦ ✦ ✦

I love the LORD because he hears my voice and my prayer for mercy. Because he bends down to listen, I will pray as long as I have breath!

PSALM 116:1–2 NLT

This is the confidence we have in approaching God: that if we ask anything according to his will, he hears us. And if we know that he hears us—whatever we ask—we know that we have what we asked of him.

1 JOHN 5:14–15 NIV

We come this morning—
Like empty pitchers to a full fountain,
With no merits of our own,
O Lord—open up a window of heaven...
And listen this morning.

JAMES WELDON JOHNSON

Delight in the Lord

Joy is perfect acquiesce in God's will because
the soul delights itself in God Himself.

H. W. WEBB-PEPLOE

✝ ✝ ✝

*Delight yourself in the LORD and he
will give you the desires of your heart.
Commit your way to the LORD; trust in
him and he will do this: He will make your
righteousness shine like the dawn, the
justice of your cause like the noonday sun.*

PSALM 37:4–6 NIV

It is not a difficult matter to learn what
it means to delight ourselves in the Lord. It is to
live so as to please Him, to honor everything we
find in His Word, to do everything the way He
would like to have it done, and for Him.

S. MAXWELL CODER

Send forth your light and your truth,
let them guide me; let them bring me
to your holy mountain, to the place where you
dwell. Then will I go to the altar of God,
to God, my joy and my delight.

PSALM 43:3–4 NIV

Our fulfillment comes in knowing God's glory,
loving Him for it, and delighting in it.

Praise the LORD.
I will extol the LORD with all my heart
in the council of the upright and in the assembly.
Great are the works of the LORD;
they are pondered by all who delight in them.
Glorious and majestic are his deeds,
and his righteousness endures forever.

PSALM 111:1–3 NIV

By Love Alone

Love does not allow lovers
to belong anymore to themselves,
but they belong only to the Beloved.

DIONYSIUS

There is an essential connection between
experiencing God, loving God,
and trusting God. You will trust God only
as much as you love Him, and you will
love Him to the extent you have touched
Him, rather that He has touched you.

BRENNAN MANNING

Find rest, O my soul, in God alone;
my hope comes from him.
He alone is my rock and my salvation;
he is my fortress, I will not be shaken.

PSALM 62:5–6 NIV

God is love. When we take up permanent
residence in a life of love, we live in God
and God lives in us. This way, love has the
run of the house, becomes at home and
mature in us, so that we're free of worry.

1 John 4:17–18 msg

✠ ✠ ✠

*By love alone is God enjoyed;
by love alone delighted in, by love
alone approached and admired.
His nature requires love.*

Thomas Traherne

Let your unfailing love surround us, Lord,
for our hope is in you alone.

Psalm 33:22 nlt

Mighty to Save

Be strong and courageous! Do not tremble
or be dismayed, for the LORD your God
is with you wherever you go.

JOSHUA 1:9 NASB

God will lift up all who have a humble spirit
and save them in all trials and tribulations.

THOMAS À KEMPIS

✝ ✝ ✝

*The LORD your God is with you,
he is mighty to save. He will take great
delight in you, he will quiet you with his
love, he will rejoice over you with singing.*

ZEPHANIAH 3:17 NIV

Whenever we touch His almighty arm,
some of His omnipotence streams in upon us...
and...through us, it streams to others.

OLE HALLESBY

By God's own free choice, He will not know
perfect happiness again till He has brought
each one of His children to heaven. He has
in effect resolved that His happiness shall be
conditional upon ours. Thus God saves, not
only for His glory, but also for His gladness.

J. I. PACKER

The most glorious promises of God are
generally fulfilled in such a wondrous
manner that He steps forth to save us at a
time when there is the least appearance of it.

K. H. VON BOGATZKY

We thank you, God, we thank you—your
Name is our favorite word; your mighty
works are all we talk about.

PSALM 75:1 MSG

See How He Loves Us!

For the LORD God is a sun and shield; the LORD
gives grace and glory; no good thing does He
withhold from those who walk uprightly.

PSALM 84:11 NASB

The beauty of the earth, the beauty of the sky,
the order of the stars, the sun, the moon…their
very loveliness is their confession of God: for
who made these lovely mutable things, but He
who is himself unchangeable beauty?

AUGUSTINE

O God, Creator of light: At the rising of Your
sun this morning, let the greatest of all lights,
Your love, rise like the sun within our hearts.

✛ ✛ ✛

*Blue skies with white clouds on summer
days. A myriad of stars on clear moonlit
nights. Tulips and roses and violets
and dandelions and daisies. Bluebirds
and laughter and sunshine and Easter.
See how He loves us!*

ALICE CHAPIN

Give thanks to him who made the heavenly lights—
His faithful love endures forever.

PSALM 136:7 NLT

Look up at all the stars in the night sky
and hear your Father saying, "I carefully set each
one in its place. Know that I love you more than
these." Sit by the lake's edge, listening to the water
lapping the shore and hear your Father gently
calling you to that place near His heart.

WENDY MOORE

Treasure in Nature

The God who made the world and everything in
it is the Lord of heaven and earth.... He himself
gives all men life and breath and everything
else.... God did this so that men would seek him
and perhaps reach out for him and find him,
though he is not far from each one of us. "For in
him we live, and move, and have our being."

ACTS 17:24–28 NIV

The longer I live, the more my mind dwells
upon the beauty and the wonder of the world.

JOHN BURROUGHS

The heavens proclaim the glory of God.
The skies display his craftsmanship.

PSALM 19:1 NLT

✝ ✝ ✝

If we are children of God, we have a tremendous treasure in nature and will realize that it is holy and sacred. We will see God reaching out to us in every wind that blows, every sunrise and sunset, every cloud in the sky, every flower that blooms, and every leaf that fades.

OSWALD CHAMBERS

Go outside, to the fields, enjoy nature
and the sunshine, go out and try to recapture
happiness in yourself and in God.
Think of all the beauty that's still left
in and around you and be happy!

ANNE FRANK

With All You've Got

GOD, our God! GOD the one and only! Love
GOD, your God, with your whole heart: love
him with all that's in you, love him with all
you've got! Write these commandments that I've
given you today on your hearts. Get them inside
of you and then get them inside your children.
Talk about them wherever you are, sitting at
home or walking in the street; talk about them
from the time you get up in the morning to
when you fall into bed at night. Tie them on
your hands and foreheads as a reminder; inscribe
them on the doorposts of your homes.

DEUTERONOMY 6:4–9 MSG

To love God, to serve Him because
we love Him, is...our highest happiness.

HANNAH MORE

✝ ✝ ✝

Love the LORD your God, walk in all his ways, obey his commands, hold firmly to him, and serve him with all your heart and all your soul.

JOSHUA 22:5 NLT

Use me, Master, in Thy vineyard.
Be the service great or small;
Keep me humble, make me fruitful—
Here's my heart, my life, my all.

MILDRED HOVER

Our prayers should be burning words coming forth from the furnace of a heart filled with love. Devoutly, with great sweetness, with natural simplicity, without any affectation, offer your praise to God with the whole of your heart and soul.

MOTHER TERESA

Ocean of Love

Dear Lord, today I thought of the words of
Vincent Van Gogh, "It is true that there is an
ebb and flow, but the sea remains the sea." You
are the sea. Although I may experience many ups
and downs in my emotions and often feel great
shifts in my inner life, You remain the same....
There are days of sadness and days of joy; there
are feelings of guilt and feelings of gratitude;
there are moments of failure and moments of
success; but all of them are embraced by Your
unwavering love.

HENRI J. M. NOUWEN

You rule over the surging sea; when its waves
mount up, you still them.

PSALM 89:9 NIV

Where can I go from your Spirit?
Where can I flee from your presence?
If I go up to the heavens, you are there;
if I make my bed in the depths, you are there.
If I rise on the wings of the dawn,
if I settle on the far side of the sea,
even there your hand will guide me,
your right hand will hold me fast.

PSALM 139:7–10 NIV

✠ ✠ ✠

*The treasure our heart searches for
is found in the ocean of God's love.*

JANET L. SMITH

Giving and Receiving

Give, and you will receive. Your gift will return
to you in full—pressed down, shaken together
to make room for more, running over,
and poured into your lap. The amount you
give will determine the amount you get back.

LUKE 6:38 NLT

It is in loving—not in being loved—
The heart is blessed;
It is in giving—not in seeking gifts—
We find our quest.

JOHN OF THE CROSS

The world of the generous gets larger
and larger.... The one who blesses
others is abundantly blessed; those
who help others are helped.

PROVERBS 11:24–25 MSG

Love is not getting, but giving. Not a wild dream of pleasure and a madness of desire—oh, no—love is not that! It is goodness and honor and peace and pure living—yes—love is that and it is the best thing in the world and the thing that lives the longest.

Henry van Dyke

✠ ✠ ✠

It is more blessed to give than to receive.

Acts 20:35 KJV

God loves us; not because we are lovable but because He is love, not because He needs to receive but because He delights to give.

C. S. Lewis

His Beautiful World

Forbid that I should walk through Thy
beautiful world with unseeing eyes:
Forbid that the lure of the market-place
should ever entirely steal my heart away from
the love of the open acres and the green trees:
Forbid that under the low roof of workshop
or office or study I should ever forget
Thy great overarching sky.

JOHN BAILLIE

Our Creator would never have made such
lovely days, and given us the deep hearts to
enjoy them, above and beyond all thought,
unless we were meant to be immortal.

NATHANIEL HAWTHORNE

The whole earth is full of his glory.

ISAIAH 6:3 KJV

If God hath made this world so fair...
How beautiful beyond compare
Will paradise be found!

JAMES MONTGOMERY

✝ ✝ ✝

He has made everything appropriate in its time He has also set eternity in their heart, yet so that man will not find out the work which God has done from the beginning even to the end. I know that there is nothing better for them than to rejoice and to do good in one's lifetime

ECCLESIASTES 3:11–12 NASB

Gifts of Love

Gratitude consists in a watchful, minute
attention to the particulars of our state,
and to the multitude of God's gifts, taken
one by one. It fills us with a consciousness
that God loves and cares for us, even to the
least event and smallest need of life.

HENRY EDWARD MANNING

Let them give thanks to the LORD
for his unfailing love.

PSALM 107:8–9 NIV

To be grateful is to recognize the love of
God in everything He has given us—and
He has given us everything. Every breath
we draw is a gift of His love, every moment
of existence is a gift of grace.

THOMAS MERTON

✛ ✛ ✛

For who do you know that really knows you, knows your heart? And even if they did, is there anything they would discover in you that you could take credit for? Isn't everything you have and everything you are sheer gifts from God?

1 CORINTHIANS 4:7 MSG

As God loveth a cheerful giver, so He also loveth a cheerful taker, who takes hold on his gifts with a glad heart.

JOHN DONNE

If you then, being evil, know how to give good gifts to your children, how much more will your heavenly Father give the Holy Spirit to those who ask Him?

LUKE 11:13 NASB

I Will Carry You

We know certainly that our God calls us to a holy life. We know that He gives us every grace, every abundant grace; and though we are so weak of ourselves, this grace is able to carry us through every obstacle and difficulty.

ELIZABETH ANN SETON

✝ ✝ ✝

Listen to me...you whom I have upheld since you were conceived, and have carried since your birth. Even to your old age and gray hairs I am he, I am he who will sustain you. I have made you and I will carry you; I will sustain you and I will rescue you.

ISAIAH 46:3–4 NIV

They travel lightly whom God's grace carries.

THOMAS À KEMPIS

He shall feed his flock like a shepherd:
he shall gather the lambs with his arm,
and carry them in his bosom,
and shall gently lead those that are with young.

ISAIAH 40:11 KJV

I could see only one set of footprints,
So I said to the Lord, "You promised me,
Lord, that if I followed You,
You would walk with me always...."
The Lord replied,
"The times when you have seen only one set
of footprints
Is when I carried you."

ELLA H. SCHARRING-HAUSEN

The Rhythm of Love

Let God have you, and let God love you—and
don't be surprised if your heart begins
to hear music you've never heard and your
feet learn to dance as never before.

MAX LUCADO

God knows the rhythm of my spirit and knows
my heart thoughts. He is as close as breathing.

✝ ✝ ✝

*Come to me. Get away with me
and you'll recover your life. I'll show
you how to take a real rest. Walk with
me and work with me—watch how I do
it. Learn the unforced rhythms of grace.
I won't lay anything heavy or ill-fitting
on you. Keep company with me and you'll
learn to live freely and lightly.*

MATTHEW 11:28–30 MSG

From the heart of God comes the strongest rhythm—the rhythm of love. Without His love reverberating in us, whatever we do will come across like a noisy gong or a clanging symbol. And so the work of the human heart, it seems to me, is to listen for that music and pick up on its rhythms.

KEN GIRE

Then those who sing as well as those
who play the flutes shall say,
"All my springs of joy are in you."

PSALM 87:7 NASB

In waiting we begin to get in touch with the rhythms of life—stillness and action, listening and decision. They are the rhythms of God. It is in the everyday and the commonplace that we learn patience, acceptance, and contentment.

RICHARD J. FOSTER

Messages of Love

The work of creating is an act of love.
The God who flung from His fingertips this
universe filled with galaxies and stars, penguins
and puffins...peaches and pears, and a world
full of children made in His own image, is the
God who loves with magnificent monotony.

BRENNAN MANNING

✟ ✟ ✟

*All the things in this world are gifts
and signs of God's love to us. The whole
world is a love letter from God.*

PETER KREEFT

Let love and faithfulness never leave you;
bind them around your neck, write them on
the tablet of your heart.

PROVERBS 3:3 NIV

True faith drops its letter in the post office box,
and lets it go. Distrust holds on to a corner of it,
and wonders that the answer never comes.

L. B. COWMAN

The sunshine dancing on the water, the sound
of waves rolling into the shore, the glittering
stars against the night sky—all God's light, His
warmth, His majesty—our Father of light reaching
out to us, drawing each of us closer to Himself.

Your beauty and love chase after
me every day of my life.

PSALM 23:6 MSG

Although it is good to think upon
the kindness of God, and to love Him
and worship Him for it; yet it is far better
to gaze upon the pure essence of Him and
to love Him and worship Him for Himself.

Love One Another

You who have received so much love share
it with others. Love others the way
that God has loved you, with tenderness.

MOTHER TERESA

Let Jesus be in your heart,
Eternity in your spirit,
The world under your feet,
The will of God in your actions.
And let the love of God shine forth from you.

CATHERINE OF GENOA

When the heart is pure it cannot
help loving, because it has discovered
the source of love, which is God.

JEAN-MARIE BAPTISTE VIANNEY

✢ ✢ ✢

*Dear friends, since God so loved us,
we also ought to love one another....
If we love one another, God lives in us
and his love is made complete in us.*

1 JOHN 4:11–12 NIV

When we really love others, we accept
them as they are. We make our love visible
through little acts of kindness, shared activities,
words of praise and thanks, and our willingness
to get along with them.

EDWARD E. FORD

Dear friends, let us love one another, for love
comes from God. Everyone who loves has been
born of God and knows God. Whoever does not
love does not know God, because God is love.

1 JOHN 4:7–8 NIV

Faithful

For great is your love, reaching to the heavens;
your faithfulness reaches to the skies.

PSALM 57:10 NIV

Faith is the assurance that the thing which God
has said in His word is true, and that God will
act according to what He has said in his word....
Faith is not a matter of impressions, nor of
probabilities, nor of appearances.

GEORGE MÜLLER

I will sing of the mercies of the LORD
for ever: with my mouth will I make known
thy faithfulness to all generations.

PSALM 89:1 KJV

It is better to be faithful than famous.

THEODORE ROOSEVELT

✝ ✝ ✝

Your love, O LORD, reaches to the heavens, your faithfulness to the skies. Your righteousness is like the mighty mountains, your justice like the great deep.... How priceless is your unfailing love!

PSALM 36:5–7 NIV

Sight is not faith, and hearing is not faith, neither is feeling faith; but believing when we neither see, hear, nor feel is faith; and everywhere the Bible tells us our salvation is to be by faith. Therefore we must believe before we feel, and often against our feelings, if we would honor God by our faith.

HANNAH WHITALL SMITH

Think on These Things

The happiness of your life depends upon
the character of your thoughts.

✝ ✝ ✝

Whatsoever things are true,
whatsoever things are honest,
whatsoever things are just,
whatsoever things are pure,
whatsoever things are lovely,
whatsoever things are of good report;
if there be any virtue, and if there
be any praise, think on these things.

PHILIPPIANS 4:8 KJV

When I think upon my God, my heart is so full
of joy that the notes dance and leap from my pen.

FRANZ JOSEF HAYDN

142

Oh, how I love your instructions! I think about
them all day long.... How sweet your words taste
to me; they are sweeter than honey.

PSALM 119:97, 103 NLT

Only to sit and think of God,
Oh what a joy it is!
To think the thought,
To breathe the Name:
Earth has no higher bliss.

FREDERICK W. FABER

Though we cannot be always thinking of God,
we may be always employed in His service.
There must be intervals of our communion
with Him, but there must be no intermission
of our attachment to Him.

HANNAH MORE

An Invitation

If you have ever:

  questioned if this is all there is to life...

  wondered what happens when you die...

  felt a longing for purpose or significance...

  wrestled with resurfacing anger...

  struggled to forgive someone...

  known there is a "higher power" but couldn't
    define it...

  sensed you have a role to play in the world...

  experienced success and still felt empty afterward...

then consider Jesus.

A great teacher from two millennia ago, Jesus of
Nazareth, the Son of God, freely chose to show
our Maker's everlasting love for us by offering
to take all of our flaws, darkness, death, and
mistakes into His very body (1 Peter 2:24). The
result was His death on a cross. But the story
doesn't end there. God raised Him from the
dead and invites us to believe this truth in our
hearts and follow Jesus into eternal life

*If you confess with your mouth that Jesus is Lord
and believe in your heart that God raised him
from the dead, you will be saved.* –ROMANS 10:9